THERE WERE MONKEYS in my KITCHEN

Sheree Fitch

Illustrations by Sydney Smith

NIMBUS
PUBLISHING

CALGARY PUBLIC

AUG   20

To my brother Shawn and sister Leanne
with memories of dancing days
in Monkey-town, New Brunswick.
—S. F.

for Mathieu, Ira, Felix, Hanna, and Esme.
—S. S.

Text copyright © 2013, Sheree Fitch

Illustrations copyright © 2013, Sydney Smith

All rights reserved. No part of this book may be reproduced, stored in a retrieval system or transmitted in any form or by any means without the prior written permission from the publisher, or, in the case of photocopying or other reprographic copying, permission from Access Copyright, 1 Yonge Street, Suite 1900, Toronto, Ontario M5E 1E5.

Nimbus Publishing Limited
3731 Mackintosh St, Halifax, NS B3K 5A5
(902) 455-4286 nimbus.ca

Printed and bound in China

Cover and interior design: Heather Bryan

Library and Archives Canada Cataloguing in Publication

Fitch, Sheree
There were monkeys in my kitchen /
Sheree Fitch ; illustrations by Sydney Smith.
ISBN 978-1-55109-994-1

1. Children's poetry, Canadian (English). I. Smith, Sydney, 1980- II. Title.
PS8561.I86T4 2013   jC811'.54   C2012-907397-0

(Text previously published by Doubleday Canada Limited, 1992, with illustrations by Marc Mongeau)

Nimbus Publishing acknowledges the financial support for its publishing activities from the Government of Canada through the Canada Book Fund (CBF) and the Canada Council for the Arts, and from the Province of Nova Scotia through the Department of Communities, Culture and Heritage.

小猴子_F1

Canada

NOVA SCOTIA
Communities, Culture and Heritage

The Canada Council | Le Conseil des Arts
for the Arts | du Canada

There were monkeys in my kitchen.

There were monkeys
In my kitchen
They were climbing
Up the walls
They were dancing
On the ceiling
They were bouncing
Basketballs

Now...
You might think
That sounds funny
Now...
You might think
That sounds neat
To see a thousand
Monkeys dancing
To a funky
Monkey beat

BUT...
Let me tell you
It was terrible
Hardest day
I ever had
I was there
So believe me
It was bad
IT WAS BAD.

First there were gorillas
In a grand ballet

Pirouette

Arabesque

Plié

Sauté

They wore ballerina slippers
And purple fishnet socks
And when they danced
The city shook
For forty-nine blocks

So…

I called the police
I called the RCMP
I was fairly polite
I even said "please"
As I shouted in the phone:

CH-CH-CH-CHIMPANZEES!

Then quicker than it takes
To do a double-duty sneeze
I turned around
And in my face
Were forty MORE...
Chimpanzees!

They wag-wiggled
They jag-jiggled
One said,
"If you please
You may call me by my proper name—
Deb-or-ah Louise."

She said,
"I am just a go-go ape
I go-go everywhere
In my red leather boots
With my punky monkey hair."

So…

I called the police
I dialed nine-one-one
I said,
"I think you'd better hurry up
THIS HOUSE HAS COME UNDONE!"

The next thing I knew
Those apes were playing rock 'n' roll
They were twisting on the table
And broke my cereal bowl

They were dancing to the Beatles
(That's an old singing group)
And they crumbled up crackers
In my minestrone soup.

Then they turned up the volume
On my brother's ghetto blaster
They got clumsy
They got goofy
They danced
Faster
Faster
FASTER

So I shouted in the phone:
"It's a

NATIONAL
    IRRATIONAL
        PRIMORDIAL
            DISASTER!"

But...

Before I had the time
To give the number
Of our street
I was interrupted rudely
By a crash—bang beat

There were fifty-five monkeys
Singing   Do-si-do!
Saying   YEE-HAW! GET DOWN!
SWING YER PARTNER
BY THE TOE!

PROMENADE!
LEMONADE!
DO-SI-DO!

They swirled and twirled
In crinolined skirts
They wore ten-gallon hats
They had rhinestones
In their shirts

So…

I called the police
I said,
"What can you do?
Has anyone reported
Monkeys missing from the zoo?"

Then…

Coming from the basement
Was a slow soft song
I peeked and saw
Orangutans
Tangoing along

They were dipping
They were slipping
They were flipping
Right out

So I got irritated and
I heard myself shout,
   "You apes have got to get!
   All monkeys have to go!"

Then they all stopped
dancing
And they shouted at me,
   "NO!"

So…

I called the police
And a security guard
I said,
   "Come get these apes!
   Get them out of my yard!"

For I'd already seen
All those monkeys on the lawn
They were playing croquet
They had gold shoes on

Some were dancing on the clothesline
Some were swinging from the trees

Hilarious

Gregarious

Chimpanzees

Then…

Coming from upstairs
Was a wheezy whining sound
So I ran right up
I took a peek
I took a look around

There were monkeys
In my bedroom
They were messing up
My quilts
One was playing
Bagpipes
They were wearing
Tartan kilts

One said,
"You can call me MacIntosh."
He did the highland fling
One said,
"Kookachica burra."
But I didn't say a thing

I just…

Called the police
And the FBI
And Scotland Yard
And a private eye

I said, "This place is CHAOS!"

I said, "BABOON catastrophe!"
You folks have got to help!
You've got to rescue me!"

Because…

Those apes had taken bubblebath
And dumped it in the tub
They played Hawaiian music
They did the hula as they scrubbed

Well…
I watched for a minute
Then I went and jumped right in it
(Don't know why…
Just thought I'd try)
But as soon as I got dry…

I called the police
I called the RCMP
I was *extra* polite
I said "Pretty, pretty *please*"
As I shouted out,
"HELP!
Ch-ch-ch-Chimpanzees!"

Some gorillas crunched granola
Some were eating toast and peas
Some were slurping macaroni
Topped with gorgonzola cheese

So I got down on my knees

I said, "This place is chaos!"
I cried, "A complete CATASTROPHE!"
I sobbed, "I want my mama!"
I sniffed, "Woe begone is me…"

So…

I went to the kitchen sink
Which is a place where I think and think (and think)
Then suddenly I had an idea
The solution to save the day
I shouted out one word:
"BANANAS!!!"
And all those monkeys stopped.

I said, "Now that I have your attention,
I'd like all you monkeys, chimpanzees, apes, and gorillas
TO GO! GET! SKEDADDLE!
HURRY UP! GET OUT OF THIS PLACE!"

Well...

One monkey came right over
One wiped my tears away
She said, "I guess that we should go
That's all you had to say…"

Then one said,
"My name is Aristotle."
One said,
"Call me Socrates."

I said,

"I'm really pleased to meet you,
Glad to know you chimpanzees."

But…

Just then I heard a siren
And I knew my help had come
There were forty-nine Mounties
They were blowing bubblegum

I said,
"This is no time for chewing
This is no time for bubbles
I tell you that this neighbourhood
Has got its share of troubles."

"I'm inspector Lee-Ann Jane,"
Said a woman dressed in red
"Can you tell us what your name is?"
"Well, uh, Willa Wellowby," I said.

"Well, Welluh Willa Wellowby
You have called us
Several times
Said you had some monkey business?
Now we're here to solve these crimes…"

Then she blew the biggest bubble
So I burst it in her face
"Look," I said, "Chimpanzees!
All over this place!"

And she said,
"Where???"

Now you probably won't believe me
But those monkeys were all gone
No monkeys in the kitchen
No monkeys on the lawn
No monkeys on the clothesline
They had left the neighbourhood

There, I thought
It's over,
I guess those apes have gone
For good.

The Inspector was not smiling
She said,
"Is this a false alarm???
Should I send you to the zoo
Or, perhaps, a monkey farm???"

I said…

"But there WERE monkeys
In my kitchen
They were climbing
Up the walls

They WERE dancing
On the ceiling
They were bouncing
Basketballs…"

"Indeed," said the Inspector.
"We do not have the time
We Mounties are too busy
We're off to solve another crime."

So…
Everything was over
No dancing apes around
I found the house a little quiet
I sort of missed the monkey sound…

But…

I think I saw an elephant
Just open up my door
And I've got this funny feeling
There are
     several
          hundred
               more

the Lovesick SKUNK

By Joe Hayes

Illustrated by Antonio Castro L.

Cinco Puntos Press
www.cincopuntos.com

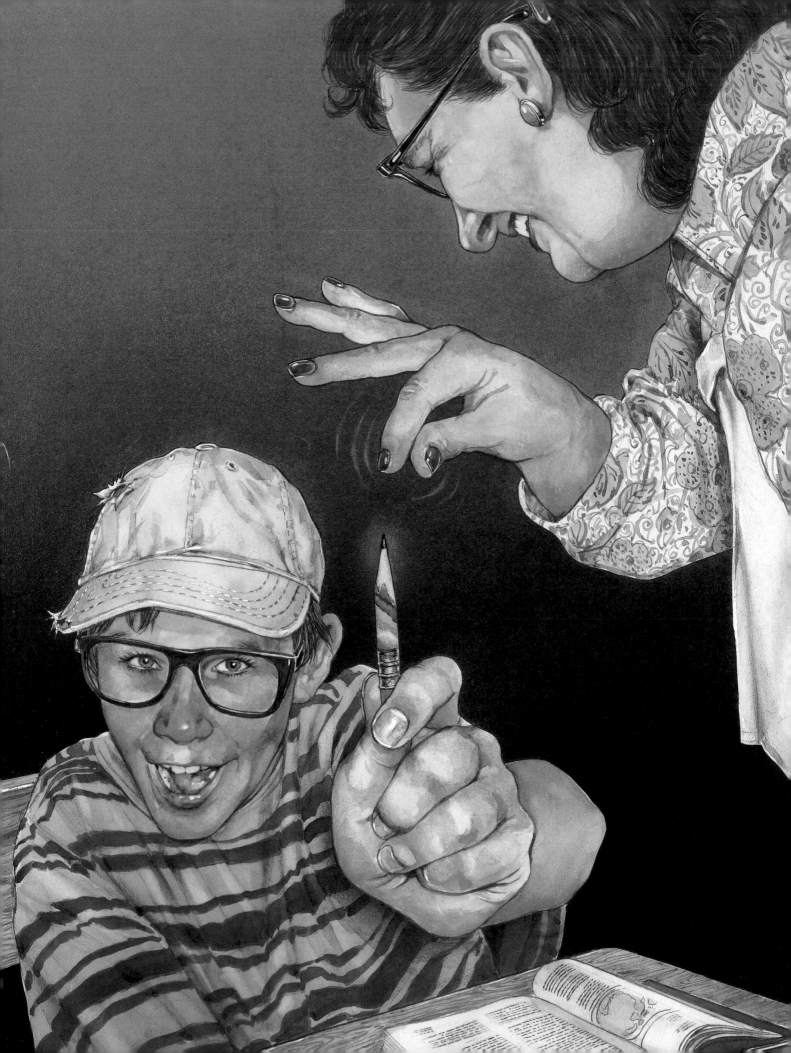

When I was a kid, I would get stuck on some simple little thing I really loved and never want to get rid of it or trade it for anything else. It might be a hat that felt just right on my head. Or a tee-shirt I'd wear until it was falling apart. Or even a favorite pencil.

Once I had a pencil with bright-colored stripes spiraling all around it—red, purple and green—with silver sparkles mixed in. The eraser was electric orange. I was the only kid in my class who had a pencil like that. I sharpened it until it got so tiny my teacher said I'd have to hold it with tweezers. "If you sharpen it any more," she said, "it's going to make invisible writing."

And once I had a pair of jeans I wore until they were so full of holes my friends called them my Swiss cheese pants. I didn't throw them away until my mom showed me they were about to get a hole in a pretty embarrassing place.

But I think the thing I loved the most was a pair of black and white sneakers. They were black high-top sneakers with a white stripe that kind of curved up from the toe to the top on each side. No one else had sneakers like mine.

I wore those shoes to school every day and to play in after school. I wore them all day long on the weekends. I wore them to birthday parties and ball games. If my mom had let me, I would have worn them to bed. And the more I wore them, the better they felt on my feet.

By the time summer came around, the laces had been broken and knotted at least twenty-five times. The sides were all tattered. One of them had a big hole in the bottom. But there was no way I would throw them away.

Every day in the summer, I'd wake up in the morning, jump back into the clothes I'd worn the day before and put on those beat up old black and white sneakers. I'd gulp down a quick bowl of cereal and head off into the desert with my good buddy Billy.

We'd spend the whole day wandering around through the mesquite and cactus or tromping through the mud and quicksand down by the little trickle of a river that ran close to our town.

Every day my black and white sneakers came home in worse shape.

But the worst thing about them was the smell! Your feet get really sweaty running around in the desert. And one day when we were running across a pasture, I stepped in a cow pie. That's not a pie cows like to eat. It's something that comes out the other end of a cow! That sure didn't make my shoes smell any better.

Another time my foot sank in some nasty smelling mud down by the river.

One day my mom met me at the door when I came home for supper. "You are not coming into this house with those shoes on," she declared and she made me take them off and leave them outside on the step.

My shoes were banned from the house, but do you think I stopped wearing them?

No way!

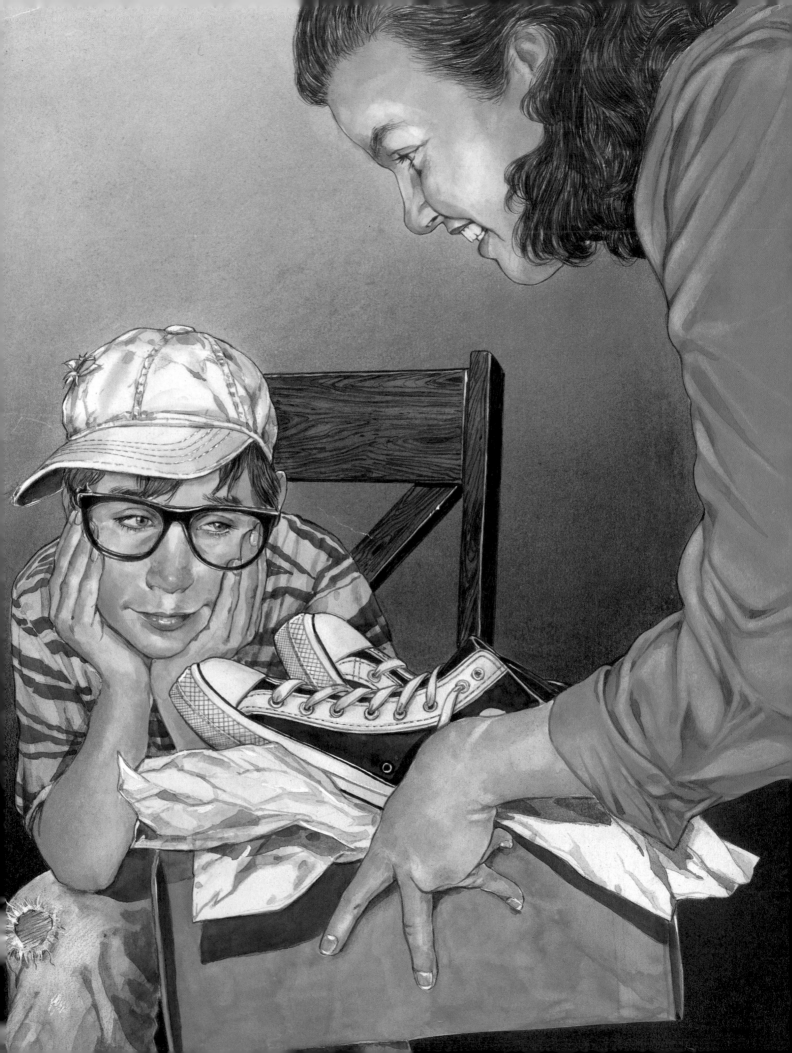

My mom bought me a new pair of black and white sneakers, just like the ones I loved. They even came from the same store. But I knew those shoes wouldn't feel the same. I didn't even try them on.

I didn't really understand how terrible my shoes smelled until the night Billy and I decided to camp out.

We had been wandering around down by the river that day and noticed a nice, grassy spot under a big cottonwood tree. We could see a circle of stones where someone had made a fire. It looked like a perfect campsite. It put the idea of a camp-out into our heads.

We headed home and asked our moms for permission and they both said it would be all right.

We packed up our sleeping bags and tent, some hotdogs and a can of beans to cook for supper, and a few odds and ends like a flashlight and some old silverware, and headed off on our big adventure.

It was already getting a little late when we got back to that big, shady tree. We pitched our tent and made a little fire in the stone circle. We cooked our supper and ate. After sitting around and poking the fire with sticks for a while, we got sleepy.

We poured water on the fire and then climbed into the tent. By that time I'd gotten used to leaving my shoes outside, so when I took them off I set them on the ground in front of the tent flap. We were pretty tired so we fell asleep right way.

But late at night I was awakened by a noise outside the tent, over by the fire circle. I found my flashlight on the floor of the tent and pointed the light over toward the fire pit. Two bright little lights came shining back at me— the eyes of some critter. And then I made out a plump black and white body. It was a skunk! A chubby little skunk.

Just about the time I shined the light on it, the skunk lost interest in whatever it was investigating over by the dead fire and started walking toward the tent. I reached over and shook Billy and he got up. We both sat there staring as the skunk got closer and closer to our tent. We were afraid to move. And then, just when it got to the door, the skunk turned around. Its tail end was pointing right at us.

We were expecting the worst!

But then we realized that what made the skunk turn around had nothing to do with us. The little skunk sidled over to my old black and white sneakers and laid its head on one of them. And then it started rubbing its cheek against them.

"Oh, my gosh," Billy whispered, "the skunk's falling in love with your smelly old shoes!"

Sure enough, the skunk started making the sweetest little purring sound—almost like a kitten—and began snuggling and cuddling up with my sneakers.

Billy and I crouched in the back of the tent staring, our mouths hanging open. We were trapped. It looked like we'd have to spend the whole night watching that skunk nuzzle against my smelly old shoes.

But a few minutes later, we noticed another movement over by the edge of the bushes. I shined the light over that way and there was another skunk. This one was huge. It was almost as big as my grandma's cocker spaniel. It came marching straight over to the black and white sneakers, pushed the lovey-dovey skunk aside and bit the toe of one of my shoes.

Then the big skunk turned around and—psssssst!—it sprayed my shoes!

The big skunk gave the little skunk the meanest look you ever saw and then turned and walked away. And my shoes' new girlfriend tagged along behind it.

My friend whispered, "That must be the little skunk's boyfriend."

Billy and I grabbed our sleeping bags in our arms and ran out of the tent holding our noses. When we got to where the smell wasn't so bad, we rolled out the bags again but we didn't get much sleep that night.

In the morning my shoes were so stinky not even I could stand them.

I waited there in my bare feet while Billy hiked back to my house to get me the new shoes my mom had bought. Then we packed everything up and headed for home. I turned and took one last, sad look at my good old sneakers. I promised myself I'd never forget them.

When I got home, my mom didn't even ask me what happened to the old shoes. She was probably so happy to see I'd finally abandoned them that she really didn't care why.

Or maybe she knew that if she asked me, I'd just come up with some wild, unbelievable story—like a run-in with a lovesick skunk and her jealous boyfriend.

THE LOVESICK SKUNK. Copyright © 2010 by Joe Hayes. Illustrations copyright © 2010 by Antonio Castro L.

All rights reserved. No part of this book may be used or reproduced in any manner whatsoever without written consent from the publisher, except for brief quotations for reviews. For further information, write Cinco Puntos Press, 701 Texas Avenue, El Paso, TX 79901; or call 1-915-838-1625.

FIRST EDITION

10 9 8 7 6 5 4 3 2 1

Library of Congress Cataloging-in-Publication Data

Hayes, Joe.
 The lovesick skunk / by Joe Hayes ; illustrated by Antonio Castro L. — 1st ed.
  p. cm.
 Summary: A boy who likes to wear his favorite clothes constantly, no matter what, leaves his smelly, black and white sneakers outside his tent during a campout and witnesses their effect on a passing skunk.
 ISBN 978-1-933693-81-1 (hardback); ISBN 978-1-941026-04-5 (paperback);
 ISBN 978-1-935955-01-6 (ebook)
 [1. Sneakers—Fiction. 2. Clothing and dress—Fiction. 3. Skunks—
Fiction. 4. Camping—Fiction. 5. Tall tales.] I. Castro López, Antonio, ill. II. Title.

PZ7.H31474Lov 2010
[E]--dc22

2010014617

Book and cover design by Antonio Castro H.

Printed in the United States of America.